CONTENTS

Acknowledgment

The author and publishers wish to thank British Telecom for their kind help in providing the information on which this book is based.

Revised Edition

© LADYBIRD BOOKS LTD MCMLXXXI

HOW IT WORKS...
THE TELEPHONE

by DAVID CAREY

with illustrations by
B H ROBINSON *and*
GERALD WITCOMB
MSIAD

Ladybird Books Loughborough

How telephones began

In every aspect of our daily lives we need to communicate with one another. We do this mostly by speaking to other people and listening to what they have to say to us, and when we are close to them we can do this very easily. However, our voices will not travel very far even when we shout, and it is thanks to the invention of the telephone that we are still able to communicate with each other and hold conversations when we are far apart.

The telephone is a method of transmitting speech by electricity. It was invented by Alexander Graham Bell, a Scotsman, who was born in Edinburgh in 1847. Bell, a teacher of elocution who later emigrated to Canada, spent all his spare time experimenting. So enthusiastic was he in his search for a means of transmitting human speech by electricity, that he left little time for his day-to-day work and at one time was almost penniless.

On June 2nd, 1875, he heard the first sounds ever to be carried over wire. Some months later in 1876 – using an instrument made from pieces of clock springs and electro-magnets – he spoke the first words ever to be sent over a distance by electricity.

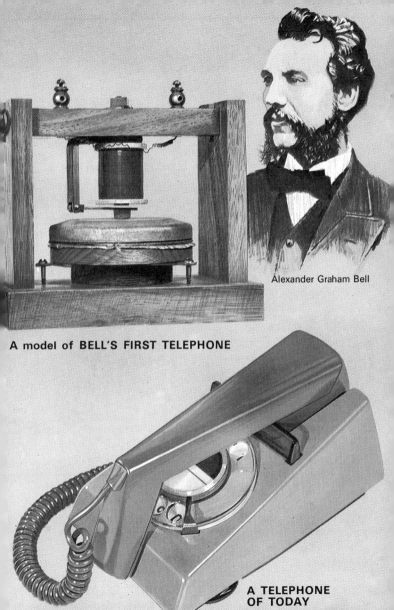

Alexander Graham Bell

A model of BELL'S FIRST TELEPHONE

A TELEPHONE OF TODAY

Although Bell had made the first telephone, at first no one seemed interested. He exhibited an instrument at an exhibition in Philadelphia but it was regarded as no more than a toy by the visitors, and almost overlooked by the judges.

Fortunately for Bell, the Emperor of Brazil happened to pass by and enquired about his invention. Bell gave him the receiver and went to speak into the transmitter at the other end of the wire. When the Emperor heard Bell's voice on the receiver, he dropped the instrument in surprise and said – "It talks". Next day Bell's invention was famous.

By coincidence, another inventor, Elisha Gray, tried to patent a telephone only a few hours after Bell had patented his. However, the Supreme Court maintained that Bell should be regarded as the first inventor even though there were many similarities between their instruments.

Another inventor, Thomas Edison, helped to make Bell's telephone even more practical by adding an *induction coil*.

The Emperor of Brazil hears Bell's voice transmitted across wires

How Edison improved on the early telephone

One of the problems of the early telephone was that transmission could not take place over very great distances. The electric current in the transmitter was small, and the resistance of the wires over which the current passed soon reduced this current to zero and made it ineffectual.

The electric current coming from Edison's transmitter was passed through a coil of wire wound round a soft iron core. This was the *primary winding*. Then a *secondary winding* was wound round. This consisted of many more turns of much finer wire. When current passes through the primary winding of such an induction coil, it causes a magnetic field to be produced in the soft iron. The magnetic field *induces* a current in the secondary winding, this current being capable of overcoming the resistance of the wires and making transmission possible over greater distances. At the receiving end Edison reversed the process, stepping down the current so that it operated the earpiece.

From the early experiments of these inventors has grown the service which the majority of us use every day. It is estimated that there are over 270,000,000 telephones installed throughout the world, nearly all of which can be connected with the instrument you have in your home, or in your locality, enabling you to have conversation with your next-door-neighbour or with someone on the far side of the earth.

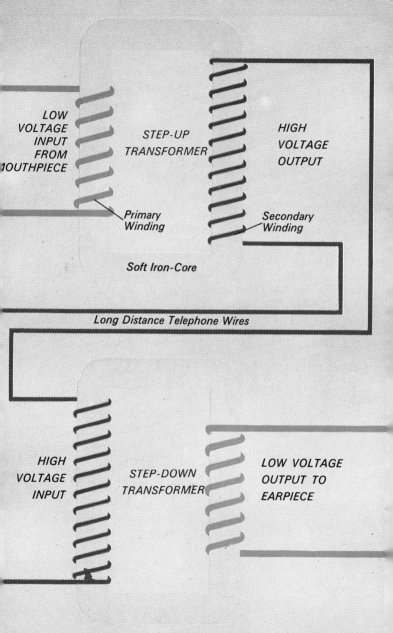

LOW VOLTAGE INPUT FROM MOUTHPIECE

STEP-UP TRANSFORMER

HIGH VOLTAGE OUTPUT

Primary Winding

Secondary Winding

Soft Iron-Core

Long Distance Telephone Wires

HIGH VOLTAGE INPUT

STEP-DOWN TRANSFORMER

LOW VOLTAGE OUTPUT TO EARPIECE

How the sound of your voice travels

When you speak, you cause the vocal chords in your throat to vibrate. These vibrations set up tiny changes of air pressure in your mouth, and these pressure changes radiate from your mouth into the surrounding air in the form of waves. Throw a pebble into a smooth pond and see how little waves of water radiate from the point where the pebble entered.

Sound waves act in a similar manner, and just as the waves in the pond diminish as they get further away from their starting point, so sound waves fade away in the air. A big pebble makes big waves in the water; a loud noise makes big sound waves in the air.

When someone speaks to you, the sound waves radiating from the speaker's mouth make an impact on your ear, a message is sent to the nerve centres of your brain and the voice is heard. If you stand too far away from the person speaking, the sound waves lose all their force, or *amplitude*, before they reach your ear and you hear nothing.

Air is not a good medium for transmitting sound waves, that is why another way of speaking to people over long distances had to be found.

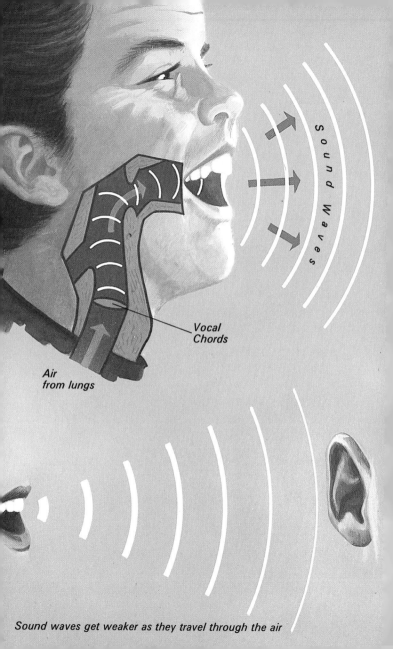

Sound waves

Vocal Chords

Air from lungs

Sound waves get weaker as they travel through the air

Sound waves into electric currents

In addition to loud sounds which cause big waves, and soft sounds which cause small waves, we also have high-pitched, or *high-frequency*, sounds and low-pitched, or *low-frequency*, sounds. A high-pitched sound, a squeak for instance, will cause the waves to radiate out very quickly one after the other. A low-pitched sound, such as a growl, will cause the waves to radiate more slowly. So, depending on how we speak and the words we use, our voices send out big or small sound waves of high or low frequency.

An electric current can be transmitted without much loss of power over far greater distances than our voices can carry in the air. What we have to do, therefore, is to convert all the changes of speech sound waves into corresponding changes of electric current which can be transmitted along wires over the required distance. On reaching the other end, the changes of electric current must then be converted back into sound waves so that the speech can be heard.

In a telephone, the mouthpiece, or transmitter, converts the sound waves of speech into variations of electric current, while the earpiece, or receiver, converts the electric current back into sound. On the next two pages we will see just how this is done.

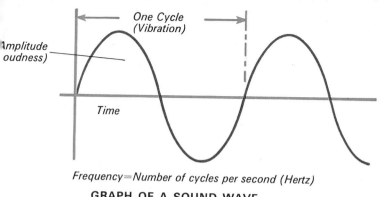

GRAPH OF A SOUND WAVE

One Cycle (Vibration)

Amplitude (Loudness)

Time

Frequency = Number of cycles per second (Hertz)

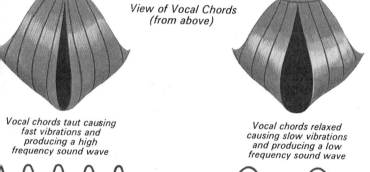

View of Vocal Chords (from above)

Vocal chords taut causing fast vibrations and producing a high frequency sound wave

Vocal chords relaxed causing slow vibrations and producing a low frequency sound wave

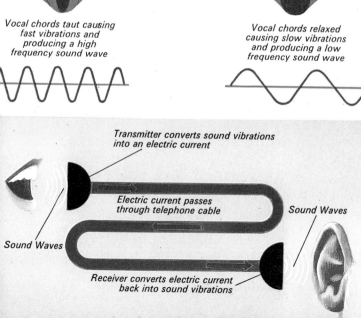

Transmitter converts sound vibrations into an electric current

Electric current passes through telephone cable

Sound Waves

Sound Waves

Receiver converts electric current back into sound vibrations

The Transmitter

The simplest and most common form of telephone transmitter consists of a thin metal disc, called a *diaphragm*, and a box containing tiny particles, or granules, of carbon which are in light contact with the centre of the diaphragm.

When you speak into the mouthpiece of the transmitter, the sound waves from your mouth cause the diaphragm to vibrate. These vibrations produce changes in pressure on the carbon granules. Big sound waves cause greater vibration and therefore greater pressure on the granules, packing them more closely together. Small sounds produce less vibration: less pressure is applied to the granules, packing them together more loosely. High-frequency sounds cause faster vibrations; low-frequency sounds cause slower vibrations. In each case the granules react in a corresponding manner.

An electric current is passed through the carbon granules and each change in pressure produces a similar change in the flow of current. The more tightly the granules are packed the greater the flow of current, and vice versa. Thus, the changes in sound waves causing the diaphragm to vibrate are converted into changes in the flow of electric current. The changes are made more quickly or more slowly according to the frequency of the sound entering the transmitter.

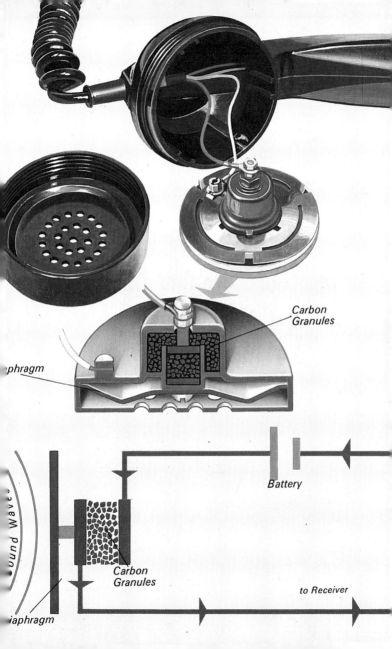

Carbon
Granules

phragm

Carbon
Granules

Battery

Sound Waves

iaphragm

to Receiver

The Receiver

The rapid changes in the flow of electric current produced in the transmitter are sent along a pair of wires to the receiver of the telephone to which you are connected.

The receiver is a metal diaphragm tightly held around its circumference and fitted close to, but not actually touching, the two poles of a strong magnet. A coil, consisting of a large number of turns of fine copper wire, is wound round the magnet. In its normal state, the magnet attracts the diaphragm with a constant pull, but when a changing electric current is passed through the coil this pull varies with the changes of current. The diaphragm is thus made to vibrate, the vibrations being in strict accordance with the current changes.

Changes of electric current created in the transmitter and passed along the telephone wires, are passed through the receiver coil and cause changes in the magnetic pull on the receiver diaphragm. Because the current changes received are identical with those transmitted, the receiver diaphragm vibrates in unison with the diaphragm in the transmitter. In this way the speech sound waves going into the transmitter are exactly reproduced by the receiver, and the words you speak at one end of the line can be heard by someone listening at the other end.

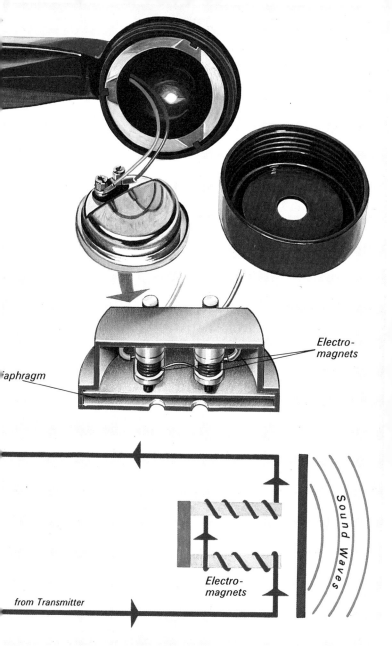

Electro-
magnets

Diaphragm

Sound Waves

Electro-
magnets

from Transmitter

Telephone exchanges

So far, we have considered a simple system in which two telephones are connected by direct lines enabling two people to speak to one another. But, of course, a great many people may want to converse with one another at any given time. By the same system of direct connection, six people would need fifteen lines while ten thousand people would require about fifty million lines. It is quite obvious, therefore, that a more practical arrangement is needed to allow a large number of conversations to take place simultaneously.

The solution to the problem is provided by telephone exchanges in which any two of the millions of telephones in daily use can be connected together. If we wish to speak to someone in a distant part of the country, or in another country altogether, our call may have to be routed through several exchanges before we can be connected with the person we want.

There used to be two main types of telephone exchange; manual and automatic. In a manual exchange an operator would make the necessary connections for us. Manual exchanges have now been phased out in favour of automatic exchanges. Automatic exchanges have equipment which will make the connections. They can be of different kinds, some working by mechanical means, others electronically.

When you make a Trunk call . . .

. . . your voice goes along cables . . .

to the local exchange and on to the . . . . . .

Trunk exchange which connects the call . .

. . through other large exchanges . . .

. . . over wires to perhaps . . .

. . . a small country exchange where you are connected to the person you have called

How manual exchanges worked

At a manual exchange, the telephone wires were connected to switchboards and, by means of short, flexible wires, or *cords*, fitted with plugs at each end, an operator could link any two telephone circuits together. Lifting the receiver of your telephone operated a switch within the instrument; electric current flowed through the circuit and lit a lamp on the switchboard. By plugging a cord into your line the operator could speak to you and you could tell her the number you wished to call. She then plugged the other end of the cord into the appropriate line and pressed a key to ring the bell of the instrument being called. When that receiver was lifted the final connection was made.

If the person you were calling was on some other manual exchange, an operator at that exchange would first be contacted. Your operator would therefore ring the second operator on a separate *junction line* and tell her the number you wanted. The second operator then made the necessary connection for you through the junction line.

A manual exchange

Automatic exchanges

In Britain today there are over 26,600,000 automatic telephones in use and the number is increasing daily. The 6½ million automatic exchanges enable you to call someone without the aid of an operator, simply by lifting the receiver and dialling the number you want. The connection between the two telephones is made at the exchange by automatic selectors, electrically controlled by the telephone dial.

We shall see how the selectors work in the next chapter, but it is important to note that they are *not* operated when each number is actually dialled *but when the dial unit returns to its normal position*. As it rotates back with the familiar 'whirring' sound, it creates current impulses corresponding to the number dialled. These impulses travel along the circuit to work *selectors*. The dialling of each number is therefore not completed until the dial has finished rotating backwards. It is important that the dial be allowed to return freely to its normal position without interference from your finger or hand.

If the person you are 'ringing' is on another automatic exchange, a special code must be dialled before the number. Dialling this code operates switches which select a disengaged junction line to the other exchange.

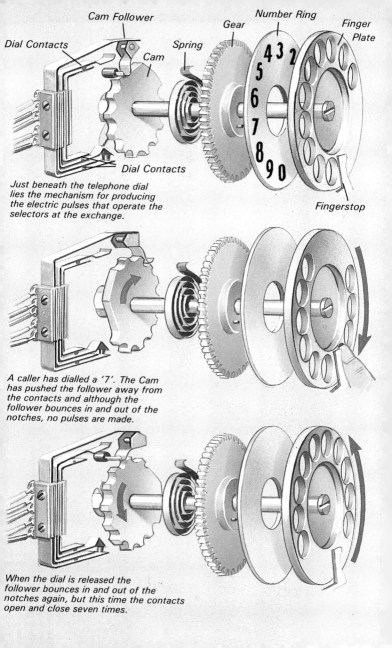

Cam Follower

Dial Contacts

Cam

Spring

Gear

Number Ring

Finger Plate

4 3 2
5 6 7 8 9 0

Dial Contacts

Fingerstop

Just beneath the telephone dial lies the mechanism for producing the electric pulses that operate the selectors at the exchange.

A caller has dialled a '7'. The Cam has pushed the follower away from the contacts and although the follower bounces in and out of the notches, no pulses are made.

When the dial is released the follower bounces in and out of the notches again, but this time the contacts open and close seven times.

How the selectors work

Each automatic telephone selector has one hundred contacts arranged in rows of ten. A switch-arm, or *wiper*, is made to move up in steps to the row determined by the impulses of the first figure dialled. The arm then passes along the contacts in that row and stops at the first disengaged one. This contact clears the way to the next numerical selector which accepts the second figure as it is dialled, repeats the process of selecting the correct row and contact, and passes the connection on to the final selector. Here the action is slightly different. On receiving the impulses of the third figure to be dialled, the switch-arm of this selector moves up to the appropriate row of contacts but does not pass along it until the last figure has been dialled. When this has been done, the arm moves along the row and selects the contact concerned. The switching operation is now complete and the telephone being called rings out automatically.

In the above description we have considered a number composed of four figures which requires three selectors. There are, of course, numbers in which five or more figures are used, in which case additional selectors have to be operated by the telephone dial in order to make the required connection.

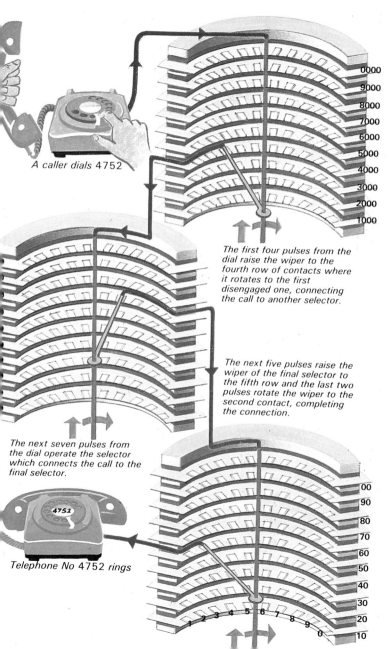

A caller dials 4752

The first four pulses from the dial raise the wiper to the fourth row of contacts where it rotates to the first disengaged one, connecting the call to another selector.

The next five pulses raise the wiper of the final selector to the fifth row and the last two pulses rotate the wiper to the second contact, completing the connection.

The next seven pulses from the dial operate the selector which connects the call to the final selector.

Telephone No 4752 rings

0000
9000
8000
7000
6000
5000
4000
3000
2000
1000

00
90
80
70
60
50
40
30
20
10

1 2 3 4 5 6 7 8 9 0

Automanual switchboards

Some day, all exchanges will work on the automatic principle, but even then there will still be a need to have some operators. Their function will still be to give assistance when we have difficulty in obtaining the number we want or when we require some special information or service. Operators will always be needed for the 'Directory Enquiry' service which provides us with the telephone number of someone in any part of the country when we only know their name and address.

These operators work at automanual switchboards which are used in conjunction with automatic exchange equipment. We can contact them by dialling numbers which are given in the telephone directories. The best known of these codes is probably 999 which we would dial in an emergency to call the police, fire or ambulance services.

The most modern type of automanual switchboard is operated by means of switches instead of cords and plugs. They are known as cordless switchboards. They can be installed in office-type rooms away from the building which houses the actual exchange equipment. The exchanges can thus be expanded when necessary without disturbing the switchboards. They are also suitable for use in small private exchanges attached to factories and other commercial undertakings.

An automanual, cordless switchboard

Dialling codes

In some areas of the United Kingdom, if you wish to call a friend *on the same exchange* you simply lift the receiver and dial the number. If he or she is in another automatic exchange area *within the same town*, you have to dial the code numbers of that exchange before the number. The codes are listed in the dialling instructions associated with the telephone you are using.

Telephones in the main cities such as London, Birmingham, Edinburgh, Glasgow, Liverpool and Manchester have been given all-figure numbers (A.F.N.) which do not include the exchange name. For instance, you might have 021-643 2107. The first series of figures represent the city, the next three figures are for the exchange and the last four, the number of the telephone. For local calls *within* one of these cities you dial the last seven figures only. The dial impulses are fed into an additional piece of equipment called a *director* which automatically directs the selection of a disengaged line to the required exchange. It then passes on the impulses of the numbers, as they were dialled, to operate selectors at that exchange.

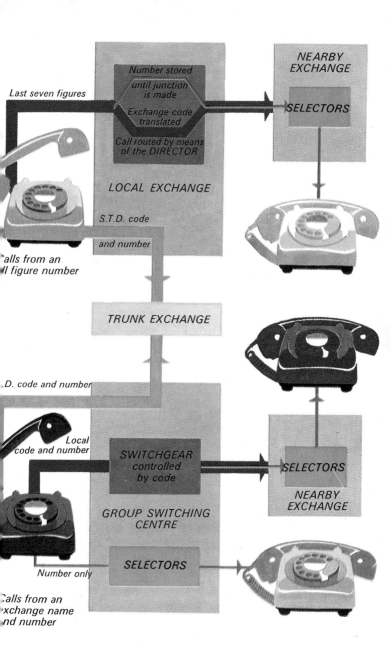

NEARBY
EXCHANGE

SELECTORS

Number stored
until junction
is made

Exchange code
translated

Call routed by means
of the DIRECTOR

LOCAL EXCHANGE

Last seven figures

S.T.D. code

and number

Calls from an
full figure number

TRUNK EXCHANGE

S.T.D. code and number

Local
code and number

SWITCHGEAR
controlled
by code

SELECTORS

NEARBY
EXCHANGE

GROUP SWITCHING
CENTRE

SELECTORS

Number only

Calls from an
exchange name
and number

Exchange systems

We have already described the principles on which an automatic exchange works, and the method by which the number dialled is selected and routed through the system. The particular equipment described belongs to the *Strowger* system which takes its name from the inventor, Almon B Strowger of Kansas City. It was first patented in the United States as far back as 1889 and was used in the United Kingdom for the first time at the Epsom exchange in 1912.

It will be seen that the system is quite an old one, yet it is still in use by British Telecom at many automatic exchanges. More recently, however, two new types of equipment have been introduced. These are called the *Crossbar* and the *Electronic* (*Reed Relay*) systems. It would take another book to describe how they work but we can learn one or two facts about them.

They are both known as Common Control systems in which information about a call is first passed to a central control point which processes it and selects the route through the exchange that the call will take. The Crossbar system works mechanically and the Electronic (Reed Relay) system is operated electronically. Both systems provide much faster connection of calls than the Strowger method.

A technical officer checking the equipment at an electronic exchange

Long distance telephoning

Until a few years ago, if you wished to make a long distance, or *Trunk* call, you always had to obtain the operator at your local exchange who then routed the call through for you. If the person you wanted was a long way away, several exchanges might have been linked together before you were finally connected.

However, new developments have now made it possible for people to dial their own trunk calls by a system known as Subscriber Trunk Dialling, or STD. This is obviously much easier, quicker and cheaper than the old method. Special apparatus known as Group Routing and Charging Equipment (GRACE for short) has been designed to interpret the instructions given by the caller when he or she dials. This routes the call through the complicated network of trunk lines to its final destination and records the charge for the call on a meter with which every telephone circuit is fitted. The telephone system is expensive to operate and every telephone conversation must be paid for according to its length, the distance it has to travel and the time of day the call is made.

To make a trunk call by STD you first dial the appropriate code then the number you want. You can find out the code by referring to the list of exchanges in the Dialling Instruction Book associated with the telephone. The code always starts with '0', which connects you to GRACE.

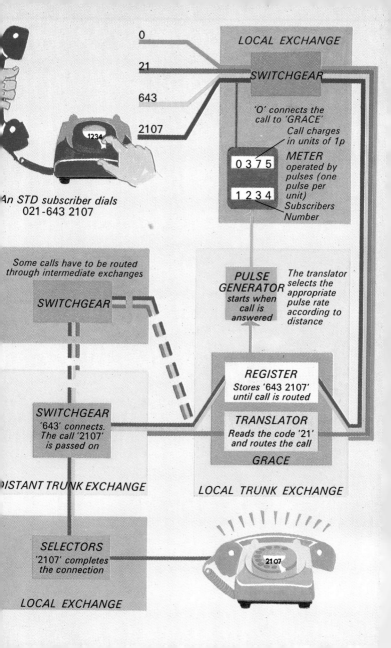

0

21

643

2107

LOCAL EXCHANGE

SWITCHGEAR

An STD subscriber dials
021-643 2107

'O' connects the
call to 'GRACE'

Call charges
in units of 1p

METER
operated by
pulses (one
pulse per
unit)

0 3 7 5

1 2 3 4

Subscribers
Number

Some calls have to be routed
through intermediate exchanges

SWITCHGEAR

**PULSE
GENERATOR**
starts when
call is
answered

The translator
selects the
appropriate
pulse rate
according to
distance

SWITCHGEAR
'643' connects.
The call '2107'
is passed on

REGISTER
Stores '643 2107'
until call is routed

TRANSLATOR
Reads the code '21'
and routes the call

GRACE

DISTANT TRUNK EXCHANGE

LOCAL TRUNK EXCHANGE

SELECTORS
'2107' completes
the connection

LOCAL EXCHANGE

Helping the electric currents over long distances

As we have said, an electric current can be transmitted over much greater distances than the human voice can travel through the air. Nevertheless, electric currents do decrease in strength as the length of wire increases. Beyond a given distance they can become too weak to do the job required of them.

This problem was partly overcome by using very thick wires which created less resistance and allowed the currents to flow more freely along them. Nowadays, long distance telephone circuits are passed through *repeaters* placed at certain points along the routes. Each repeater boosts, or amplifies, the current passing through it, before sending it on to the next repeater where it is amplified again. In this way the losses of strength are made good and the current reaching the end of a long line is as strong as if the line were short.

The amplifying of the currents at the repeaters was done by thermionic valves and, more recently, by transistors similar to those used in our television and radio sets. These devices enable us to carry on telephone conversations over great distances, not only within our own country but by submarine cables and radio links to all parts of the world.

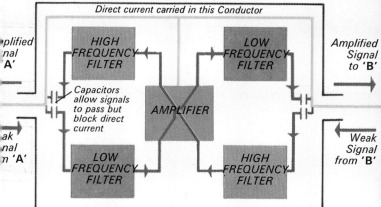

A Submarine Cable has Repeaters at intervals of about 30 miles

Repeater Casing

Direct current carried in this Conductor

Amplified Signal to 'A'

HIGH FREQUENCY FILTER

LOW FREQUENCY FILTER

Amplified Signal to 'B'

Capacitors allow signals to pass but block direct current

AMPLIFIER

Weak Signal from 'A'

LOW FREQUENCY FILTER

HIGH FREQUENCY FILTER

Weak Signal from 'B'

Repeater contains filters which allow conversations to flow in both directions in a single cable. Conversations in one direction are transmitted in a lower frequency band, while those in the other direction are transmitted in a higher frequency band.

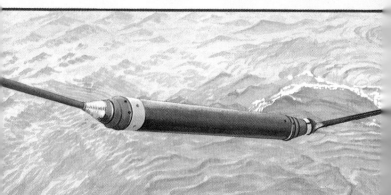

A SUBMARINE REPEATER *going overboard from a Cable Ship*

International services

Today we are able to have a telephone conversation with someone in Europe, or much further away, almost as easily as we can speak to a friend in the next street. Thanks for this are largely due to the submarine cables laid by cable ships of British Telecom and other cable companies.

The idea of undersea cables is not new. The first was laid as long ago as 1891 between St. Margaret's Bay in Kent and Sangatte in France. It had only four wires, and only two conversations could be carried on at the same time. Many cables of much greater capacity are now in use and we can talk to any European country at will. Six cables run under the Atlantic Ocean between Europe and North America. Others connect San Francisco with Sydney (Australia) and Wellington (New Zealand) by way of Hawaii and Fiji. Extensions to Commonwealth countries in South East Asia were laid between 1965 and 1967.

The laying and maintenance of these long distance cables is very expensive. They may become damaged by the movement of tides, currents, rocks, ships' anchors and the trawls of fishing vessels. When a fault is reported, a cable ship is sent to the area, the cable is located by special instruments and then dragged up by grapnel to be repaired.

LOADING CABLE INTO A TANK OF A CABLE SHIP

LIGHTWEIGHT SUBMARINE CABLE (Cut away to show its component parts)

Polythene Insulation

Conductor

Steel Centre Cable for Strength

'Return' Conductor Tape

Aluminium Screening and Signal Conductor Tape

Cotton Tape

Polythene Sheath

Radio-telephones

The kind of telephone systems we have been considering up till now are those in which two telephones are directly connected by a pair of wires, or the equivalent, even over distances of many thousands of miles. We can now consider a method whereby the wires terminate at a radio station and the greater part of the distance is covered by radio waves.

The year 1927 saw the first radio-telephone service opened between Great Britain and the USA. Today, radio communication is available with most countries of the world outside Europe, and with many suitably-equipped ships at sea.

Normally, ships can be contacted up to a distance of about 250 miles by a medium-range radio-telephone system operated through British Telecom Coast Radio Stations. Larger ships can be reached all over the world by means of high-powered radio stations, providing the ships have the right kind of equipment. British Telecom has also developed a transmission technique known as *Lincompex* which greatly improves the clarity of speech transmitted by short-wave radio.

At much closer range, police patrol cars are in constant radio-telephone contact with their control rooms, whilst many business-men and women and members of the government are able to talk to their offices while travelling by car.

Opposite (above): A British Telecom Coast Radio Station (below): A ship's officer making a radio-telephone call from a ship at sea

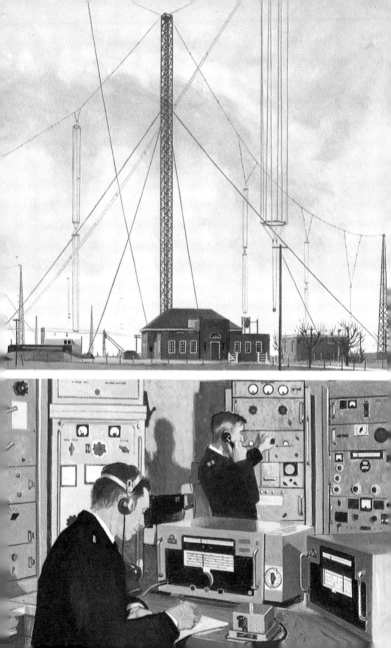

London Telecom Tower

We live in an age of technological change, and the technology of the telephone is becoming more advanced every year. There are over 17,000,000 exchange lines in use in the United Kingdom and these carry over 20,000,000,000 calls a year.

Some of the extra circuits required are provided on existing cables by the use of a system known as *Pulse Code Modulation*, or P.C.M. With this system, thirty calls can be made at the same time over two circuits. New *co-axial* cables are able to carry as many as 127,400 simultaneous calls. In future, the existing copper or aluminium conductors will be replaced by optical fibre cables. Also, radio microwave networks will operate through 160 stations located in various parts of the country. In this system, high-frequency radio waves are beamed between directional dish or horn-shaped aerials erected within visible contact of one another.

In the British Isles, the main centre for all these activities is the London Telecom Tower near Tottenham Court Road. Six hundred and twenty feet in height, this is one of the tallest buildings in the United Kingdom and so gives the radio beams an unobstructed path. The dish and horn-shaped aerials can, at one time, deal with 150,000 telephone calls and provide 50 television channels.

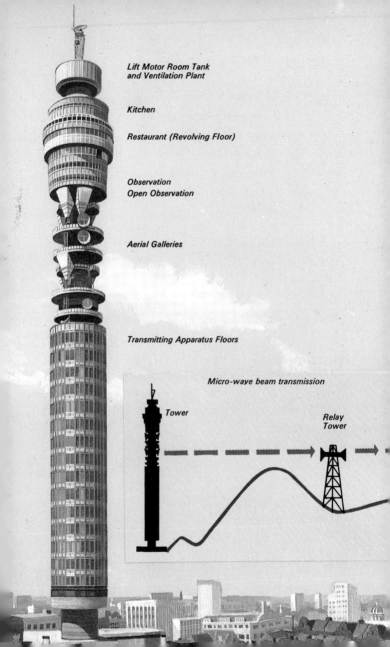

Lift Motor Room Tank
and Ventilation Plant

Kitchen

Restaurant (Revolving Floor)

Observation
Open Observation

Aerial Galleries

Transmitting Apparatus Floors

Micro-wave beam transmission

Tower

Relay
Tower

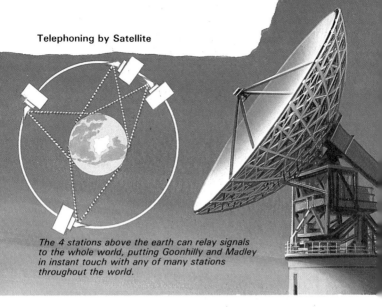

The 4 stations above the earth can relay signals to the whole world, putting Goonhilly and Madley in instant touch with any of many stations throughout the world.

Telephoning by Satellite: Earth Stations

A large number of international telephone calls are transmitted via one of the communications satellites which are now keeping station above the Earth. Satellite services are provided in Britain through the 'earth station' at Goonhilly Down, in Cornwall. In November 1978 a new earth station was brought into service at Madley, near Hereford. Between them Madley and Goonhilly link Britain by satellite with more than 70 countries.

Goonhilly sprang into fame when it was used in the first transatlantic television programme made via the satellite, Telstar, in 1962. The equipment was later modified to take part in a regular commercial satellite communications service across the North Atlantic by way of the 'Early Bird' telecommunications satellite. The station has been in constant operation ever since.

The UK is the second largest user of the Intelsat communications satellite systems. British Telecom provides service through three Atlantic satellites to North and South America, Africa and the Middle East and through the Indian Ocean satellite to places as far east as Hong Kong, Japan and Australia. There are three 90 foot aerials and one 62 foot aerial at Goonhilly which handle telephone calls, satellite communications and data and television transmissions. At Madley there are 3 dish aerials operational.

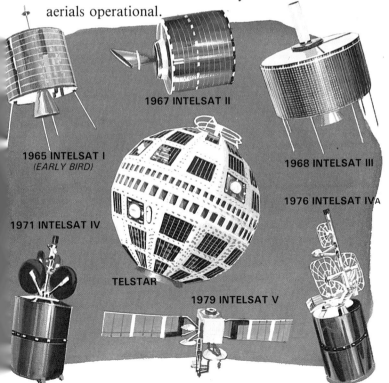

1967 INTELSAT II

1965 INTELSAT I
(EARLY BIRD)

1968 INTELSAT III

1976 INTELSAT IVA

1971 INTELSAT IV

TELSTAR

1979 INTELSAT V

Special Services

Having a telephone in our homes not only allows  es and business people any country abroad, but ole range of special

hese are:

Keeping Time
The Speaking Clock can help you by giving the time correct to one twentieth of a second.

Alarm Calls
An alarm call can be booked through the operator, preferably the evening before, for early morning calls.

Weather
Check with the Weather Phone for information supplied by the Meteorological Office.

Motoring
Call the Motoring Phone for information supplied by the AA, covering roads within 50 miles of each centre.

Recipes
Call Dial-a-Recipe for daily recipes provided by cookery experts.

Gardening
Get advice and gardening tips from an expert by calling the Gardening Phone.

Dial-a-Disc

Two different hit records are played each night from 6 pm to 8 am Monday to Friday. Five different records are played on Saturday and Sunday.

Cricket

The Cricket Phone gives state of play during Cornhill Insurance Test matches played in England, and other major competitions.

What's On

A daily selection of the main events in London is provided by the British Tourist Authority.

Skiing

This service details skiing conditions at the principal Scottish ski centres during the skiing season.

Bedtime Stories

A story written and recorded by a well known children's story-teller is available from 6 pm each night.

Santa Stories

Seasonal stories for children available all day during the Christmas period.

Greetings Telegrams

Messages for special occasions can be given to the operator and will be delivered by hand on appropriate greetings cards.

Business News

The Financial Times industrial ordinary share index is updated 7 times daily, Monday to Friday, along with a summary of business news items. After 10 pm a stockmarket report, company news and tomorrow's Business Diary are given.

Information on how to find the available services is contained in the telephone directory covering the area concerned.

Emergency services

Of course, one of the important functions of the telephone is to provide us with a method of obtaining help when we need it. The emergency telephone system is there for this purpose and we are able to call on the police, fire and ambulance services at a moment's notice. Also, in appropriate areas of the country, we can summon up the coastguards or mountain and cave rescue teams. Calls for these services are free.

Emergency calls can be made from most telephones by dialling 999, although in some areas you may have to dial 100 or 0 instead. Instructions on which code to dial are fixed to the telephone you are using. An exchange operator is always available to answer an emergency call and he or she will need to know the service you want, and your telephone number in case you have to break off the call for some reason. When the particular service answers, you must give all the information you can so that they will arrive at the scene, with the right equipment, as quickly as possible.

The emergency services are there to help us when we need them urgently. If you wish to contact them on a non-urgent matter, ring their normal telephone number. Special facilities are provided at one mile intervals along motorways. These boxes are painted blue and are available for calls to the motorway emergency patrol services only in case of breakdown or accident.

Public services

The first telephones for use by the general public were usually installed in shops. Call boxes (the modern name is call offices) made their appearance on the streets in the early 1900's and, because there were several independent telephone companies in operation at that time, the boxes were a varied collection of shapes and colours. British Telecom telephone kiosks of a standard colour and pattern were introduced in 1921.

In the British Isles there are now more than 77,000 public telephone kiosks, cabinets and booths in operation, and they can be used for local or trunk calls and for sending telegrams. The methods of making calls from these offices vary according to the area and the type of exchange equipment in use, but suitable instructions are printed on notices near the telephone. Most kiosks now have pay-on-answer STD facilities. You should try to have enough of the right kind of coins with you before you telephone so that you can insert them in the coin box and so avoid having the call cut off in the middle of a conversation. Emergency calls are of course free, as they are when made from private telephones.

CALL OFFICE 1908

KIOSK No. 1 1921

Learning more about the telephone

There is one kind of telephone we have not yet mentioned, that is, the *Videophone*. This is rather a special sort of instrument, still in the process of development, but it could well be the normal system in years to come. The videophone is really a combined telephone and television which enables the person speaking to actually see the person he or she is speaking to. It will be just like talking to someone in the same room with you.

If you have read this book you will now have a very good idea of how the telephone works and of all the equipment and systems which go to make up a complete, world-wide telephone service. You may be satisfied with the information we have been able to give you in these few pages. On the other hand, you may be technically-minded enough to want to go into the subject in greater detail or even make the telephone service your career. In either event, British Telecom will be pleased to give you advice on the technical books available and the steps you can take to further your education.

One way of learning more is to visit a telephone exchange. With what you have already learned, it should be a very interesting and instructive experience. Arrangements can be made by contacting your local Telephone General Manager's Office (Service Department).

Telephone tones

Telephone tones are signals which give you information about the call you are trying to make. They are quite simple and easy to recognise.

DIALLING TONE A continuous purring sound, letting you know that the exchange equipment is ready for you to dial. It is useless to dial before you hear this tone.

RINGING TONE 'Burr-burr' repeated regularly tells you that the dialled number is ringing out. If there is no answer after a reasonable time, replace the receiver and try again later.

ENGAGED TONE A single, high-pitched note repeating at regular intervals. This normally indicates that the telephone you are calling is already in use. It can also mean that there are no free lines at the exchange. Replace the receiver and try again in a few minutes.

NUMBER UNOBTAINABLE TONE A steady note. This means the number you have dialled is not in use. Check that you have dialled the correct code and number and try again. If you get the same tone, call the operator and explain what has happened.

PAY TONE Rapid pips mean that you are being called from an STD coin-operated telephone. You must then wait for the caller to insert the money – when the pips will stop – before he will be able to hear you.

Speaking on the telephone

Some people are not used to speaking on the telephone and sometimes become nervous when they have to do so. Others who